DATE									
OCT 2 0 78.	FEB 7 '90	MAY 4 - 2003							
NOV 1 7 '78	MAR 12 '90								
DEC 1 5 78	NOV 20 '90								
JAN 26 '79	MY 3 '01								
JUN 23 '79	MAY 24 2001								
AUG 1 - '79	MAR 2 1 2002								
MAY 4 '88									
AUG 4 '88									
SEP 2 0 '88									
SEP 26 '88									
FEB 10 '89									

SUBJECT TO LATE FINE

THE PIG
WHO COULD CONJURE
THE WIND

BOOKS BY SHIRLEY ROUSSEAU MURPHY

The Grass Tower
Silver Woven in My Hair
The Ring of Fire
The Pig Who Could Conjure the Wind

by *Shirley Rousseau Murphy*

DRAWINGS BY MARK LEFKOWITZ

Atheneum • *New York*

1978

THE PIG WHO COULD CONJURE THE WIND

Library of Congress Cataloging in Publication Data

Murphy, Shirley Rousseau.
    The pig who could conjure the wind.

SUMMARY: A witch pig's one passion in life,
to fly on the wind, is seriously endangered when
a demon puts a spell on her.
    [1. Pigs—Fiction.   2. Fantasy]   I. Lefkowitz,
Mark.   II. Title.
PZ7.M956Pi   [Fic]   77-20512
ISBN 0-689-30639-3

Text copyright © 1978 by Shirley Rousseau Murphy
Illustrations copyright © 1978 by Mark Lefkowitz
Published simultaneously in Canada by
McClelland & Stewart, Ltd.
Manufactured in the United States of America by
The Book Press, Brattleboro, Vermont
Typography by Mary M. Ahern
First Edition

To Beth Johnson

S.R.M.

To Shari and David
and my family with love

M.L.

Chapter 1

Now in Sooeee Hollow there lived an old pig, beyond the falls, in a house by herself and tumbled down. And she wore a pair of coveralls. And she was a witch.

She was a rough-bristled, big-footed pig, with wee yellow eyes and a vague and dreaming expression. Her ancient coveralls were tattered and frayed. She lived quite alone, with no one to love her, and only one passion in life: To be up in the wind and away.

Her name was Miss Folly, and a witch she was. For Miss Folly could conjure the wind. Make it blow or die aborning, or tumble and twist like a wild thing. And more—Miss Folly could ride that wind.

Oh, it was fearsome and wonderful to see her carried high aloft and tumble and swing on a gusting breeze. Pigs would gather from miles around to call out advice and to ask her for favors and tricks.

"Fly upside down, Miss Folly!"

"Do a spin! A slow spin!"

"Somersault, turn a somersault!" someone would cry as the pigs of Sooeee Hollow stared upward.

"Shhh, child, don't yell at that witch."

"Oh, Ma! Somersault! Somersault!"

But Miss Folly paid them no mind. She would ride out over the sea on a storm cloud, black, till she was only a speck in the sky. Then she would come a-riding back with the thunder rolling and the lightning flashing around her.

There in the wind she was free. Nothing could catch her, nothing could hurt her, nothing could bring her down. And there from the sky she could see, far from Sooeee Hollow, the world of incredible humans, see baseball games and baby carriages and ice cream wagons, hat shops and carpenters and small gray cats. She could hear all the sounds of the city, horns honking and symphony concerts and children screaming in the play yards, and she could hear the bells.

Oh, how Miss Folly loved bells.

Sooee Hollow had no bells; but when she flew away over the city, she could hear the bells of trains and fire engines and trolleys; and on Sundays the

church bells rang. Miss Folly loved, better than life itself, to hear mighty church bells ring, to float over the spires of a Sunday morning and hear the great bells clanging.

But that was only on Sundays.

On weekdays she would leap on a fast little breeze and whip off to the city park. There, from the sky, she could watch all the people as they ate their picnic lunches, chased dogs, changed diapers, tied shoelaces and read their daily newspapers. She thought it all very grand, and she wished she could join

them there. But Miss Folly was far too shy.

One afternoon as she looked down on the park, another wind came careering; not a tame breeze like Miss Folly's, but a gale, strong and dark and fierce. It spun wildly over the heads of the people, snatching up books and turkey sandwiches and making the babies cry.

A laugh came from that wind, a terrible chortle, and there was a demon on top with an evil look in his eye.

"Go away!" cried Miss Folly. "Get away from here. You don't belong in this park!"

The demon ignored Miss Folly, swooped, screaming with laughter, and jerked off an old lady's hat. "Stop it!" cried Miss Folly. "Stop at once. Who do you think you are!"

The demon laughed in her face, made his wind whirl, and whisked up a little black dog. He set the dog on a billboard where it began to howl, then he turned over trash cans, shouting with glee, and whipped the trash around the park until it hung like snow on the trees.

Miss Folly's wind shivered and turned to run, but Miss Folly would not let it go.

The demon's wind dipped, spun like a top, and sucked up a very small boy. It went careering off with him, still on his trike, over the rooftops, the boy yelling out with amazement.

Miss Folly followed fast. She saw the boy go bump on a chimney and thump against an antenna. The demon's laugh was terrible, and he smelled of fire and hot places. He looked back once, and his eyes flashed with pleasure and he shook little Edward Gotz—that was the boy's name, Edward Gotz—who hung onto his trike with one hand and waved happily down at his mother. She, poor woman, was frantic.

The demon swooped again, picked up a cat, and the cat dug his claws into Edward. The demon snatched up a goat, and the goat bleated madly and Miss Folly followed faster.

The demon plucked a lineman from the top of a pole, and the lineman shouted with fear. He had never been so high, not up in the sky, not in his forty-two years! Edward Gotz, astride his trike, with cat clinging, looked around with surprise and wondered why the lineman was so pale.

Well the demon's wind rose higher. It grew blacker. The lineman turned quite green. The cat's claws dug deeper, the goat hid his head and Edward stood up on his handle bars, drunk with the joy of it all.

Miss Folly came thrashing on. Her wind bucked like a bronco. "That demon'll drop them, he'll drop them for sure! Or take them to Heaven knows where!" She cried out a spell, and her wind leaped ahead as she clung for all she was worth.

Oh, what a ride! The demon's wind flew so terribly fast that lineman, cat, Edward and goat were nothing more than a blur. The demon's laugh shook the sky as he headed for the open sea, and Miss Folly knew if he dropped them there, it would be a long swim home.

"Stop!" she demanded and gestured and muttered and made her wind go faster still till she was only a streak in the sky.

She drew close to the demon at last. She said a spell to the demon's wind. The demon's wind began to falter, and the demon screamed with fury as he dangled Edward, lineman, cat and goat low over the salty waves.

Miss Folly shouted her most powerful spell. The demon's wind shivered. She made wonderful signs with her hooves, and the demon's wind trembled and shook. She beckoned at last, and the demon's wind came to her, docile as a wind could be.

"Put them down on that field," cried Miss Folly. "Put them down gently, you wind."

The demon seethed with indignation. He cried out a spell, too, but his wind paid no attention. It swung close to earth, and it set its passengers down, and the demon simply bellowed with rage.

The knoll was grassy. It was smooth. The cat looked around and began to wash. The goat began to graze. The lineman fainted dead away, and Edward Gotz looked up at the sky and wished he were flying there still.

"Now," cried Miss Folly as she raised her old hooves, "Come here, you wind, and take up this demon and carry him so far away he'll never be seen again!"

The wind darkened. It roared. It plucked up the demon and carried him off—but just before he was whisked away, the demon shouted a spell. A terrible spell. He put a curse on Miss Folly that was horrid.

"You will not," he cried, "you will not, from this day, ever fly when the bells start to ring. Bells will make you fall, you hoyden old pig, quickly and firmly to earth!

"Ringing bells will make you fall!"

Chapter 2

Poor Miss Folly. The demon's curse was a terrible thing. She flew on home feeling awful. She got into bed without supper, still wearing her coveralls, and dreamed of bells and of falling and of the demon laughing at her.

She woke quite unhappy, with bags under her eyes, nervous and cross and depressed. *Could* it really be true? *Would* bells make her fall?

There was only one way to find out.

On the next Sunday morning she swept up and away on a quick little breeze until she hovered over the spire of the First Methodist. She heard organ music and the Sunday sermon and the sweet voices of the choir and was transported with joy as the music rolled up all around. She listened, treading wind, smiling and utterly content.

Then the organ thundered its very last chord. The people began to file out. And as Miss Folly looked down to admire the starched dresses, the bells rang clear and loud.

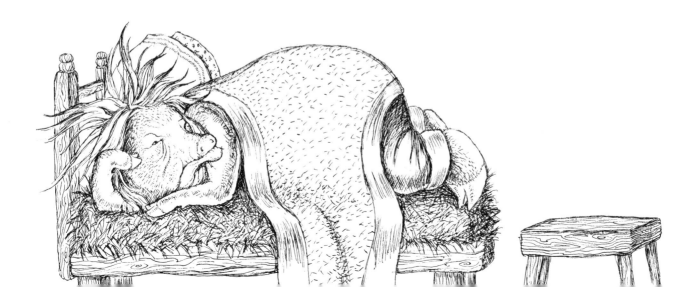

When they stopped ringing, she was upside down in the top of a tree, stuck all over with chestnuts and twigs, frightened and bruised and chagrined.

She went on home where she belonged and was very good for a while. But Miss Folly missed the bells badly. To see a train far away like a small black snake made her yearn to fly after it. To think of a bike or a trike or a bright fire engine made her unbearably sad. And on Sundays when she could hear the far church bells, Miss Folly stayed grumpily in bed.

The pigs of Sooeee Hollow tried to cheer

her. They baked her cakes and invited her to parties and stopped her on the street to talk.

But Miss Folly refused to be cheered.

She wished she'd never laid eyes on that demon. She was utterly, completely unhappy, and her friends could do nothing for her.

Then one Sunday morning she could stand it no longer. She knew she must try once again. Maybe the curse had worn off. She would fly to the church before the bells rang and would sit on the roof, very still. She called up her wind and off she flew. And the sky was clear and the city below her was sunny.

She did not get as far as the church. As she banked in low over the surrounding houses, the bells rang clear and long. Miss Folly fell in a heap. She landed on a balcony and lay limp.

Cut out this scene?

The door to the parlor stood open.

Beyond was a fine apartment.

At last she picked herself up. She felt of her bruises and sniffed back a salty tear. And when she sniffed back that tear, Miss Folly inhaled an utterly delicious smell. It came from the open door. She stopped her crying and pricked up her ears and her interest in life returned. Whatever did she smell?

It might be a pot pie. Or perhaps a ragout. Or maybe it was curry and rice.

Miss Folly rose up on her old splayed hooves and pushed her nose shyly at the door. Could she just take a peek? Who would care? Everyone was surely at church.

She eased past the lace curtains, past the potted ferns and into the little parlor. The floor was carpeted in red, the furniture was satin and polished wood and the chandelier was crystal. Miss Folly was very impressed.

She took a long breath, slipped into the kitchen and stood on the tips of her toes. There on the stove was a golden brown crust, fluted and deep and oozing juices. She had just stuck out her tongue to take a taste, when a screech made her freeze in terror.

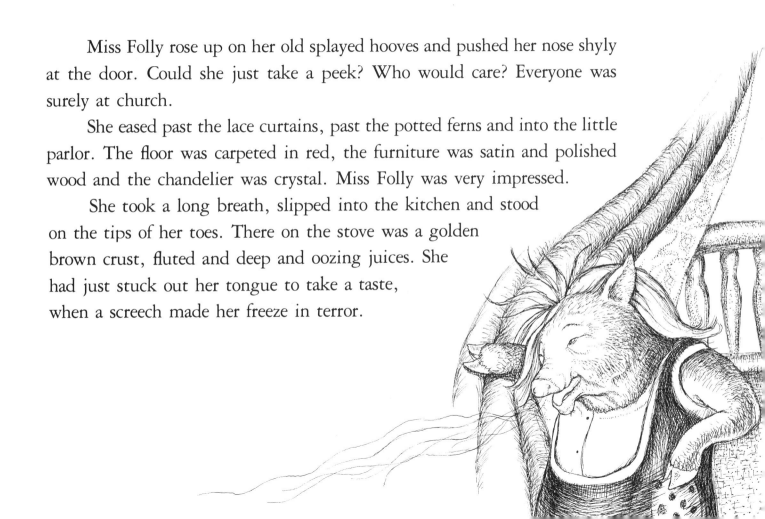

"*Pig! It's a pig!*" cried a high little voice. Miss Folly spun around, forgetting the pie, and there in the corner, in a cage rocking madly, was a corpulent yellow canary. "*It's a pig in the kitchen! Piginthekitchen!*" cried the frantic bird.

Miss Folly was horrified.

She spun again, confused and befuddled as the demented bird shrieked and rattled. And there in the doorway, blocking her exit, stood the biggest cook she had ever seen, and surely he was the fiercest. He stared hard at her. "Why it's a pig in my kitchen! And a pig is the next thing to roast pork!" He grabbed up the butcher knife and began to chase her as the canary shouted, "*Roastpork!*"

"*Roastpork! Roastpork!*"

Miss Folly circled the kitchen. She doubled back with the cook hard on her heels. She knocked over a chair, saw the butcher knife swing, and ran

straight between the cook's trousered legs. She called for her wind and it came blowing. It slammed through the door and she leaped aboard, careered through the parlor a foot off the floor, and flew out the door like a hurricane.

"Oh!" sighed Miss Folly when she finally got home, "I'll never go near a bell again, never!"

Well her vow lasted exactly one week. And this time, oh, the trouble it caused was the worst she had ever encountered.

Chapter 3

On a fine Sunday morning in Sooeee Hollow, in her house tumbled down, Miss Folly heard church music sweet on the wind, forgot her vow, straightened her coveralls, called up a breeze, and rose into the bright morning sky. She flew off over the hills and was soon peering down at the lifting spires of St. Theresa's.

One small dome window stood open. She gazed down through it at the burning candles and the heads of the singing people. A little unease stirred

Miss Folly. A little voice whispered, *You are too close.* But Miss Folly chose not to listen.

The colored windows gleamed. The prayers rose up. The singing was fine. Miss Folly hovered enraptured.

Then the bells rang. Miss Folly fell between the domes, screaming, and landed atop the church roof. The bells clanged and resounded as she scrambled and squealed. Her hooves slid on the roof tiles, and she slipped down across them toward the one open window in the dome.

She hit the sill with a thud. "Oh!" cried Miss Folly. "Someone help me!" But of course no human could understand the frantic cries of a pig. She clung half in the window, half out, lamenting mightily.

The sound of her squealing was terrible as it echoed in the church below.

She turned her eyes to Heaven, but no help could be seen.

She turned her gaze downward, to the terrified people and only frightened faces looked back. All but one. One frail old man peered up at Miss Folly with wonder.

Miss Folly slipped. She clung to the sill. The priest ran down from the altar and stared up at her. The bells clanged loud and long, and the organ echoed Miss Folly's cries.

And then she lost her hold. Miss Folly fell tumbling through space. Her cries rose as she twisted, and the colors from the windows reflected on her sides so she looked like an Easter egg falling down from the roof of the church.

The children's choir whispered, *"Falling angel!"* But the adult congregation knew Miss Folly was something a whole lot worse. Some people jumped up, others fainted, and others crowded to the aisles.

"It's a devil!"

"It's an imp!"

"It's a fiery fiend come to punish us!"

Miss Folly wanted to say she was none of these things, but she was far too busy falling. Besides, pigs can't talk to people. The bell ringer, upset by the din, pulled harder and harder on the rope, making a terrible agitation.

"It's a spawn of darkness!"

"A denizen of Hell!"

"No it's not, it's an angel!" cried the members of the children's choir.

"An angel? Oh no! Look at its face, it's quite evil! And who *ever* saw an angel in coveralls!"

"It's a pig!" cried a small boy. "It's only a pig, can't you see!" Yes, the boy was Edward Gotz.

"A pig! Don't be silly!" cried the congregation. "It's a devil and we must destroy it!"

"But it *is* only a pig," whispered the old man. No one heard him, though. And at that moment Miss Folly fell with a thud straight into the old man's lap.

She peered up into the old man's face. He looked back at her. "Be still," he whispered. "Be quiet, and maybe I can save you."

But Miss Folly was too upset to be still. She raised her nose in anguish and screamed long and mightily.

"It's a devil all right!" cried the people.

"IT'S ONLY A PIG!" shouted Edward.

"Shhh," said his mother. "That's ridiculous."

The old man rose painfully. He
hoisted Miss Folly, and she was heavy for
him, for he was lame and frail and bent.
He carried her out toward the aisle,
nonetheless, trembling under her weight.
"Let us pass!" he said, thrusting forward.
The crowd drew back, but the voices were
loud behind him. He reached the door
and stepped into the morning with Miss
Folly safe in his arms.

He limped down the street. Miss Folly
clung to him. Edward Gotz ran alongside,
and just before the boy was jerked

away by his mother, he whispered in the old man's ear, an urgent secret.

Calls of *"Devil!"* followed them.

"Devil! Devil!"

Miss Folly felt so dismayed. She hadn't meant to cause trouble. Couldn't they see she was only a pig and could do no one any harm! She had only wanted . . . and here a tear started. She had only wanted . . . another tear fell, and another. The old man patted her cheek.

The old man carried Miss Folly to his little cottage and sat her down in his favorite chair. He poked up the fire and made her some cocoa and then he began to cook dinner. He limped back and forth between table and stove, stirring pots and setting out plates. And when at last they were seated at the dinnertable, he said the blessing, then looked at Miss Folly with wonder.

"You flew there, to the roof of that church. How amazing!"

Miss Folly blinked in answer.

"What a wonderful thing. But the bells made you fall, Edward told me. He said it was the curse of a demon."

Miss Folly shuffled her feet.

"You love the bells," he said sadly. "It was the bells that drew you, and the demon knew that. What a terrible curse to have made."

Miss Folly nodded and another tear started—but this was a tear of pure joy. For no one, not even in Sooeee Hollow, not in Miss Folly's whole life, had ever understood how happy the bells made her feel.

At last the old man rose. He hobbled to a shelf, wound up a Victrola and put a record on. And a wonderful music began, a beautiful din that had bells in it and trumpets and more. It swelled and surged like the wind swells, and it carried Miss Folly's spirit aloft as the wind had carried her old bony self.

When the music was done, Miss Folly sat hearing it still in her head. She was quite engulfed by it. What could she do for this kind old man that would be half as fine a gift?

At last she led the old man out the cottage door. The evening sky was pink. Miss Folly called up a gusting south wind, and she took the old man on her back. She carried him up on that wind, up into the wild free sky. And that old man, crippled and lame, was set free. On Miss Folly's back he sailed without effort or pain across the endless sky. The air was fresher. The trees and hills and houses were spread out like toys below, and the old man swung free on the sky's great waves and wished he need never come down.

Chapter 4

The evening was growing dark when they landed at last in the center of the cottage garden. A band of townspeople was waiting for them, and it pressed in close around.

"They were flying!"

"No natural pig can fly! It's a demon, I say! A demon!"

"It's only a pig!" cried Edward.

"A devil's pig!"

"Or a witch!"

"*A witch in pig's clothing!*"

"We'd better lock it up before it makes more trouble!"

"She hasn't made *any* trouble!" cried Edward.

"Catch the pig before it gets away!"

"The old man too! He must be the witch's familiar!"

"It's only a pig and a poor old man and they haven't bothered *you!*"

No one paid attention to Edward.

They grabbed the old man by his beard and Miss Folly by her coveralls and hauled them to the jail. They locked them up there and stood staring in at them through the bars.

"There must be a trial! Try the pig for a witch and the old man for its familiar!"

"And for flying! They have to be tried for flying!"

When the people grew tired at last of staring and accusing and began to think fondly of their Sunday night suppers, they straggled off home, leaving the old man and Miss Folly in the cold stone cell without any supper at all.

A supperless Sunday. A cold, uncomfortable night. And for breakfast someone brought them stale bread and water, which they shared out equally.

Miss Folly sighed and looked at the old man. It was not his fault he was there.

The old man sighed and looked back at Miss Folly. What would become of them?

They had licked the bowl clean when they began to hear voices coming through the little cell window. "It's the trial," shouted someone. "The witch's trial. Hurry so we'll get a good seat!"

"Everyone's going!"

"It's only a pig and a harmless old man," cried a small familiar voice.

"Where is the judge?"

"He's coming."

"Will they be found guilty?"

"Of course!"

Miss Folly stared at the old man and he stared back, and it was a dark Monday morning indeed.

Chapter 5

When the pigs of Sooeee Hollow heard about the trial, they decided to attend. They dressed in their best and went out between the cliffs and across the hills to the city.

The city dwellers had never seen so many pigs at one time, dressed in their best or otherwise, and they lined the streets and stared. Children ran alongside, and one little girl gave a young pig a licorice, which made his face all smeared.

A fine procession of pigs. The sun shone down on them as they neared the courthouse. Forty stone steps led up. The pigs climbed them two by two. The double doors stood open, and inside was a marble hall. The pigs crossed it two by two. The people all followed them. The courtroom doors stood open, and the courtroom was dim and still. The pigs entered two by two.

The walls were panelled with gleaming wood, the ceiling was high, the judge's bench was tall and carved. From his chambers came the judge, his black robe flowing, and everyone stood up. The judge seemed very impressed by the number of pigs who were present.

Miss Folly looked with amazement at the pigs from Sooeee Hollow and thought they were there to laugh. But then she saw their faces. They were there because they loved her! Oh, love was a wonderful thing!

"Face the front!" cried the bailiff.

Miss Folly turned toward the judge. But she dared not look up at him. She could only stare downward, at her old splayed hooves. The clerk read the crimes with which they were charged, and it was an awesome and frightening moment.

Miss Folly was accused of being a witch and of flying in church, and the old man was accused of complicity.

What was complicity? Miss Folly wondered. She really had no idea.

"It's like collusion," the old man whispered, seeing her expression. But that didn't help at all.

"*Was* it collusion?" asked the judge.

"I don't believe it was collusion," said the old man uncertainly.

"Did you ride on a flying pig, old man?"

Now the old man was confounded. If he said *yes* he would admit that Miss Folly could fly. If he said *no* he would be lying.

The judge held up his hand and withdrew the question, and turned instead to Miss Folly.

"Pig, were you flying in church?"

Miss Folly shook her head from side to side for she had not been flying in church.

"Were you *in* the church?"

Miss Folly nodded miserably and tears began to roll down her bony nose.

"Pig, can't you speak?" asked the judge.

"She cannot talk to people," said the old man.

"Then you must speak for her. *Was* this pig in church?"

"She was," said the old man truthfully.

"She was flying!" someone shouted.

"She's a witch!" someone else cried.

The voices rose. The judge pounded. The pigs of Sooeee Hollow grunted loudly. The judge's face grew red. He beat and beat with his gavel, the bailiff demanded order and finally the crowd was stilled.

At that moment, Edward Gotz entered the courtroom.

He was followed by the lineman, by the goat, by the cat. He had left his tricycle at home. The judge stared at him, everyone stared at him, people and pigs alike.

Chapter 6

Edward Gotz looked up at the judge. The cat and the lineman edged closer together, and the goat began to nibble the clerk's robe. Edward Gotz spoke very clearly. "She didn't fly in church," he said. "Your Honor, she fell in."

There was amused laughter behind him because Edward Gotz was only a small child so how could he know anything.

The judge glared at the tittering people.

"Fell in?"

"Yes, sir. She fell through the little window in the dome."

"And she cannot fly?"

"Oh, she can fly," admitted Edward. "It's the bells make her fall, you see. She didn't fly *in* church, not once."

"She flew above the church, and the bells made her fall!" The judge seemed impressed by this.

"That's right, Your Honor," said the old man hastily. "The boy is telling the truth. She didn't mean to fall through the window. She just wanted to hear the music and see the people and listen to the bells when they rang."

"And when the bells rang she fell," repeated Edward, staring up at the judge's stern face.

The judge scowled down at Miss Folly, at Edward, at the goat and the lineman, who both seemed quite shy, and at the cat who twitched his ears in agreement and looked back without blinking at the judge.

And the judge began to smile. "A pig who can fly!" he shouted. "Why it's a wonder and a miracle, a stupendous miracle! What are we trying her for!"

"For being a witch," whispered the clerk.

"Well," said the judge, looking down at Miss Folly, "*are* you a witch, old pig?"

Miss Folly nodded in dismay.

The judge looked at the old man. "How long have you known this witch?"

"Since Sunday morning, Your Honor."

"Did you help her in any way?"

"I carried her from the church and gave her Sunday dinner."

"That is no crime. Is that all?"

"I played some music for her."

"Nor is music a crime," said the judge. "Old man's case dismissed!" And he turned, then, to Miss Folly. "But this pig admits to being a witch, so I must find her guilty of that. I sentence you, pig . . ." And here he paused for a long time. The courtroom was very still. One little pig whined with concern and was immediately hushed.

Then the judge spoke at last. "I sentence you, pig . . . *for life!*"

Miss Folly's old heart sank to her toes. She stared at the judge in dismay.

"For life," said the judge. "For as long as you live, you will be keeper of the windows of St. Theresa's."

Miss Folly gazed up at him, bewildered.

"Keeper and polisher of the windows. It is a difficult task for a person to wash those high church windows. But for a flying pig it should be as easy as getting out of bed in the morning. Every Saturday you will wash the church windows. Each little pane of glass. And no bell shall ring, ever, by order of this court, no bell in town shall ring while you fly there. Not of a Saturday."

Miss Folly was overcome.

"And every Sunday morning," continued the judge, "you shall attend the holy services, and no one will speak unkindly to you."

Miss Folly's tears simply flowed down her old bristly face.

So every Saturday morning for the rest of her life Miss Folly rose before dawn, ate a big breakfast, called up her wind and flew off to the Church of St. Theresa.

She began at the bottom and worked her way up, polishing each little colored pane, polishing birds and trees and clouds and the faces of the saints, all with a very soft cloth. And she did it with wonderful joy, rising higher and higher upon her breeze until she reached the highest windows in the dome. And never once, while she polished, did the bell ringer pull on the rope.

And every Saturday morning Edward Gotz would ride on her back as she polished, as high as his mother would allow (which was never high enough, nor quite as exciting as that wild ride on the demon's wind).

Then every Sunday morning for the rest of her life Miss Folly would tie an apron over her coveralls, put on a bonnet, enter the church through a proper door and sit in a proper pew.

And after church every Sunday the old man would take Miss Folly home. He would fix her dinner and play her some music; then Miss Folly would call up the wind.

It would come sweeping into the old man's garden, and off they would go over the rooftops, over the trees, over the running children who played and shouted below them. Over the dogs and the trucks and the little green parks. Over the land they would fly, just the two of them, the old man and the old white pig from the house tumbled down, beyond the falls, dressed in bonnet and apron and coveralls.

the end